Megan

"It's a tattoo," said Lily. "Only it's in two halves. I'll have half of it, and you have the other half, Megan. Look, it says 'For Special Friends'."

Make Friends With
Megan
Ann Bryant
ORCHARD BOOKS

Chapter One

"Are you ready, Megan?" came Cally's voice up the stairs.

It was Saturday afternoon. Megan was in her room. She was sitting on the corner of the bed with her knees bunched up. She'd pulled her dark hair over her face. Her mum and dad were both working this weekend, so Cally, the nanny, was in charge of her and her little sister, Beth.

"Megan!" shouted Cally. "Time to go now!"

Megan pretended not to hear. But a moment later Cally was at the bedroom door.

"Come on, you naughty little madam. Open the curtains," she said, pulling Megan's hair off her face. Then she picked her up and carried her to the top of the stairs as though she was a toddler. She was trying to make Megan smile.

Megan didn't feel like smiling. "Let go of me. I don't want to meet Jules in town," she said crossly, as she slid out of Cally's grasp.

"You'll enjoy it," said Cally, holding Megan's hand firmly.

Megan stomped downstairs beside Cally. "I won't enjoy it because you and Jules will keep chatting to each other and I'll be stuck looking after Beth. That's what happened last time."

"Ssh. Beth's asleep in her buggy," said Cally, as they reached the hall.

"She'll wake up when we get to the park," said Megan. "She always does. One little quack from a duck and she'll be magically wide awake!"

Cally laughed and winked at Megan. "You're right there, Megs. I think your little sister understands duck language better than English!"

Megan was quite pleased that Cally thought she'd said something clever and funny, but she wasn't going to smile. No way! She was still cross about having to meet Jules. Jules was a new friend of Cally's – a very talkative one.

Cally wheeled the buggy gently outside and turned to Megan with a secretive look on her face. "Jules is bringing someone with her this time."

"Oh great!" said Megan, scowling. "That'll make it even worse!"

"No it won't," said Cally, smiling as they set off down the road, "because the person Jules is bringing with her is her niece. She's called Lily and she's the same age as you. So what do you think of that!"

Megan couldn't help feeling the teeniest bit interested. But she wasn't going to let Cally think she'd stopped being cross.

"What if I don't like Jules' niece?" she said. "Just because she's my age doesn't mean I'm going to like her. She's probably horrible and mean and she might even hate me."

"I think you're getting carried away now," said Cally. "Jules says Lily is a real sweetie."

"Do you want me to eat her then?" asked Megan grumpily.

And that made Cally laugh like mad. "You're such a funny girl!" She ruffled Megan's hair and all the bangles on her wrist jangled.

Megan was looking forward to when *she* was old enough to wear loads of jangly bangles. She sighed. She'd probably have to wait a while yet. Her mum was quite strict about things like clothes and jewellery. Whenever Megan was going to a party, her mum always wanted her to wear a dress. Megan wanted to wear trousers with a really nice bright top and glitter in her hair.

"There they are," Cally suddenly said. "Outside the café!"

Megan looked. Jules was wearing tight jeans and a white top under a shiny white jacket. As they got nearer Megan saw a big red ruby in Jule's tummy button. But where was Jule's niece?

And just at that moment a small girl came out from behind Jules. She had straight brown hair. Her shoulders were hunched up as though she was cold and her face looked very white, with freckles. She glanced quickly at Megan and Cally, then looked down at the ground.

She doesn't look much fun, thought Megan. I bet she's good all day long and doesn't like anyone who's even a teeny bit naughty. That means she won't like me.

"Nice one, Jules!" said Cally, rushing up to Jules and poking her in the tummy.

Jules and Cally hugged each other.

Megan stood there holding on to

Beth's buggy and feeling silly and cross because she didn't know what to say and Cally seemed to have forgotten about her. It was going to be just as bad as Megan thought. And probably worse too.

★★★

Chapter Two

"Have you said hello to Megan, Lily?" asked Jules.

Lily looked quickly at Megan and then back at the ground, but she didn't speak.

I was right, thought Megan. Lily doesn't want to meet me. And I don't want to meet her either. It was a stupid idea of Cally's.

"Come on, I'm dying for a coffee," said Jules, pushing open the café door.

They sat down at a table right in the middle. Beth was still fast asleep. Cally ordered the drinks.

"And a plate of cakes, please," she said to the waitress.

Then Cally and Jules leaned their elbows on the table and started talking. Lily moved her chair so she was very close to Jules.

How boring, thought Megan. She wished the cakes would hurry up and come. Eating would be better than doing nothing.

"Want get out!" said Beth, waking up suddenly, and pushing her tummy against the buggy straps.

"I'll get her out," said Megan, jumping up. At least there was something to do now.

Cally was so busy nattering to Jules

that she didn't even notice that Beth had woken up.

As Megan sat Beth on her lap the cakes and drinks arrived. The very second the waitress went, Beth grabbed a chocolate éclair and crammed it in her mouth.

"No!" said Megan sternly to Beth as she tried to get the éclair out of Beth's hand. "Cally! She's getting covered in chocolate!" But Beth squeezed all the tighter and cream oozed between her fingers and blobbed down her T-shirt.

"You little monster!" said Cally, looking in horror. "Give it to me, Beth."

And that was when Megan looked across the table and saw Lily grinning all over her face. Megan was surprised. She thought Lily would think Beth naughty. Beth saw Lily's grin too and laughed

delightedly. She slapped both her chocolatey hands on the table and laughed again.

Megan held her little sister's arms tight to her body so she couldn't make any more mess. But Beth made herself very thin and floppy, then slithered out of Megan's grasp and on to the floor. Then, before Megan could stop her, Beth had grabbed the bottom of the tablecloth.

"No!" Cally screeched as Beth tugged.

The glass of Ribena toppled over, splashing Lily's face and top.

"Oh Beth!" cried Jules and Megan, jumping up from their chairs.

Lily just sat there, looking shocked. Megan waited for her to be cross. If someone had made Ribena splash on to Megan's face she would have gone mad. But Lily just wiped her face with a paper napkin and started to giggle.

Beth was having a great time. She decided to march round the café and entertain *everyone*. As she marched she sang at the top of her voice, to the tune of *The Wheels on the Bus,* "The ice cream wafers go oosh, oosh, oosh!"

And that's when Lily's giggles turned into a great big laugh. Megan was about to tell her it wasn't funny. But when she met Lily's eyes, she found that it *was* funny. *Very* funny. The two girls kept grinning at each other and laughing more and more until the tears were running down Megan's face. And as Megan laughed she wondered what ever had made her think that she wasn't going to like Lily.

Chapter Three

"What's your favourite colour?"

"Purple."

"So's mine."

Lily and Megan were pushing Beth's buggy. They were walking in the park, with Cally and Jules behind them. Since they'd left the café, Megan had found out that Lily was two months older than her, had one brother of five, one sister of eleven and a hamster called Tricky. Lily had also told her that she was always shy until she got to know people.

"Jules is really my auntie because she's my mum's sister," Lily explained, "but she doesn't seem like an auntie so I just call her Jules. She often looks after me and my brother and sister if Mum's at work."

"Where are your brother and sister at the moment?"

"My brother's at his friend's house and my sister's playing in a netball match."

"Ducks!" Beth suddenly called out, loudly.

"She loves feeding the ducks," Megan told Lily.

Opposite the pond, on the other side of the path, was a grassy slope.

"Look!" said Megan to Lily. "Let's climb up there!"

"You be careful," said Cally, taking Beth out of her buggy.

"Come on," said Megan, because Lily

was looking at the hill as though it might bite her.

When they got to the top, Megan had an even better idea. "Shall we roll all the way down?"

Lily's eyes grew round. "Won't your mum be cross if you get grass stains on your clothes?" she asked, in a voice that was half worried and half excited.

Megan looked down at her brand new T-shirt. It was true, her mum *would* be cross, but now she'd got the idea of rolling down, she just had to do it.

"I don't think we'll get any grass stains. Come on!"

Lily giggled as they lay down on their sides.

"Wheeeeee!" they screeched, as they rolled faster and faster.

"Cool!" said Jules. "If I hadn't got my

white top on I'd join in!"

For the next ten minutes Megan and Lily rolled down the slope again and again, laughing their heads off. It was after the tenth roll that Megan noticed the green marks on her jeans and her top. She spat on her finger and rubbed the spit into one of the marks to see if it would come off, but it stayed just as green as before.

Lily bit her lip and stared at the marks on her own clothes. "D'you think we'd better stop now?"

"No, it's too much fun," said Megan. "Anyway it won't make any difference if we get a few more marks now we've got so many."

Lily's eyes sparkled as she followed Megan back up the hill.

Finally Cally said that it was time to go.

Megan was just about to ask when she

could play with Lily again, when Jules said, "See you guys on Monday."

"Are we coming to the park after school?" asked Megan excitedly.

"No, we're going shopping."

"Wicked!" said Megan, giving Lily a thumbs up sign.

Lily's pale face broke into another wide beam. "Yeah, wicked!" she agreed.

When Megan and Cally were walking back home with Beth in her buggy, Cally said, "So, what did you think of Lily?"

"She's nice," said Megan, feeling a big bubble of happiness inside her.

"Really?" said Cally, with a cheeky grin. "So she wasn't mean and horrible after all?"

Megan didn't say anything but she went pink.

Chapter Four

As they walked home Megan looked down at her T-shirt and started to get anxious. It was daubed with chocolate where Beth had wiped her hands on it in the café. But the chocolate was nothing compared to all the thick green streaks on her T-shirt, her jeans and even her trainers. She suddenly realised something. The fun was over now and the crossness was about to begin.

Maybe Mum will still be at work,

thought Megan. Then I can get changed and put my clothes in the wash before she sees.

But Megan's heart sank when she saw her mum's car was outside the house.

Cally had her own key. She let them all in.

"I'm dying for the loo!" said Megan, darting past her and dashing upstairs.

"Hello," said her mum, coming into the hall. "Have you had a good day?"

"I'm just going to the loo," called Megan, diving into the bathroom at the top of the stairs.

"What's that green stuff all down your back, Megan?"

"Nothing," Megan called.

When Megan looked over her shoulder at the back of herself in the bathroom mirror, she gasped, there were so many

grass stains. She waited a few seconds, then rushed into her bedroom. She peeled off her T-shirt and jeans and put on some leggings and a sweatshirt. Then she wrapped the jeans and T-shirt in a little ball and stuffed them into the back of her wardrobe. She'd put them in the wash later when she was sure her mum wasn't around.

In the kitchen, Cally and her mum were chatting and Beth was sitting in her high chair eating some bread and butter.

"I'm afraid she made a right mess with the chocolate éclair," said Cally. "She'd grabbed it before anyone noticed."

Megan's mum laughed but pretended to be cross with Beth. "You're a pickle, aren't you! Hm!" Then she saw Megan

standing there. "Why have you changed, Megan?"

A really good answer popped into Megan's head. She didn't look at Cally when she said it.

"Beth put her chocolatey hands all over my other clothes."

"Oh dear. You'd better get them and put them in the wash."

"I'll be off," said Cally. "See you on Monday, Megs." She gave Megan and Beth a quick kiss and said goodbye to their mum.

Megan came downstairs with her clothes still rolled up in a ball. She peeped through the crack in the kitchen door and saw that her mum was getting something out of the cupboard. Quick as a flash, Megan popped the clothes in the washing machine, then started talking in a rush.

"I've got a new friend, Mum. You know Cally's friend, Jules? Well it's her niece. She's called Lily and she's two months younger than me and she's got a brother and a sister and a hamster called Tricky and she's got orange hair and freckles and she's really nice and... can she come to tea one day?"

Megan's mum laughed. "I don't see why not. I'll have a chat to Cally about it."

Megan smiled to herself. What a brilliant day it had turned out to be!

★★★

Chapter Five

After school on Monday, Cally, Megan and Beth were going up the escalator in a big shop in town. Cally had decided to leave the buggy in the car as Beth always liked walking in shops.

They were meeting Jules and Lily in the ladies' clothes department. Megan was very excited.

The moment they got to the top of the escalator, Megan spotted Jules trying on a jacket. Lily was busy watching

Jules so she didn't see Megan creep up behind her.

"Guess who?" said Megan, covering Lily's eyes with her hands.

Lily jumped. "Megan!" she said, sounding delighted.

"How did you know!" laughed Megan. Then she turned to Cally. "Can we choose my top first?"

So they went through to the children's department, Cally holding Beth's hand tightly, while Beth pulled and pulled and tried to get away.

"Stop it, Beth!" said Cally firmly. "You've got to hold my hand or you'll get lost."

The top that Megan liked the best was pale blue with a big '15' on it all in red studs. She really wanted it, but she knew her mum would say it was too old for her.

"Wow!" said Lily. "That's really cool."

Now Megan wanted the top more than ever because Lily liked it so much.

"This is the only one I like, Cally."

Cally looked doubtful. "I don't think your mum will approve," she said. "What about this one?" She was holding up a white top with tiny yellow flowers on it and puffed sleeves.

Megan saw Lily wrinkle her nose. That decided it. "Mum *will* like this one. Honestly," she said, handing the pale blue top to Cally and trying not to go at all red.

Cally was still looking doubtful, but she went off to pay for it.

"Jules!" said Lily, sounding very excited. She was looking at some tattoos. "Can I borrow eighty-five pence, and I'll pay you back with my

pocket money when we get home?"

"What do you want to buy?" asked Jules.

"It's a tattoo," said Lily. "Only it's in two halves. I'll have half of it, and you have the other half, Megan. Look, it says 'For Special Friends'."

Megan stared at the two halves of the knot. It was the most brilliant idea she'd ever heard. And she felt so happy that Lily thought they were special friends.

The moment Jules had paid for the tattoos the girls unpeeled them. They'd decided to put them on their arms just above the elbow. Jules helped them both to stick them on so that when they stood side by side with their shoulders and arms touching, the two halves of the knot joined up and looked like a whole knot.

Megan thought it was the best present she'd ever been given.

"Ooh, that's nice nail varnish!" said Cally, eyeing a stand that was covered with little bottles and pots.

"Duck!" cried Beth, toddling off on her wobbly legs.

"Oh no you don't, young lady!" Cally said, scooping her up.

"Duck!" Beth repeated, pointing to a stand with bags on it. Sure enough there was a mini backpack in the shape of a duck. "Feed ducks!" said Beth. And everybody laughed.

Megan was looking at all the pots of nail varnish.

"Can I try some on?" she asked Cally.

"Well, just be careful you don't spill it," said Cally.

"I'm going to look at the shoes over

there," said Jules. "Back in a mo."

"Come back here, little Miss Runaway!" said Cally, chasing after Beth again, who was running towards the duck bag as fast as her little legs would carry her.

"I'll do your nails for you, Megan," said Lily. "What colour do you want?"

"I'll have a different one on every nail," said Megan.

Lily unscrewed the bottle of sparkling mauve, but suddenly stood still, with the brush in mid air.

Her eyes went big as she whispered, "Look, Beth's made all those bags topple on to the floor! Will Cally get into trouble?"

"There's the shop lady going over to talk to her," said Megan.

"Oh no!" said Lily in a high squeak.

"I've dropped nail varnish on your skirt!"

Megan looked down to see a little blob of sparkling mauve, with a neat dotty trail going down from it.

"Quick, have you got a tissue?"

Both girls searched their pockets, but could only find a chewing-gum wrapper in Lily's coat pocket. Megan grabbed it and started rubbing her skirt. She watched in horror as the neat little blob turned into a nasty big smudge.

"Put it in the wash when you get home," said Lily.

"But this is my school skirt. Mum'll go mad!"

"Maybe nail varnish remover will work on clothes." Lily's eyes looked enormous in her pale face as she nodded at Megan. "I bet it will."

Megan decided to forget about the

smudge. She was desperate to see her nails coated in sparkly varnish. "Never mind," she said to Lily, as she separated her fingers and stretched them out. "Have another go. Start with my thumbnail."

This time Lily didn't spill any. The brush wobbled quite a bit though, so the mauve varnish went on her thumb too. The girls giggled as Lily did Megan's second fingernail in gold, the third one in green and the fourth one in silver.

It was when Lily was in the middle of putting dark blue on Megan's little fingernail that Cally's voice behind her made her jump. A thread of blue trailed from the brush right across Megan's hand.

"This little sister of yours nearly got me in big trouble," Cally said. "Luckily no damage was done. Ooh! You've

made a mess of the blue, haven't you? Never mind, it'll come off with nail varnish remover."

Cally hadn't noticed her skirt. But her mum would. Megan got that horrible feeling again, that the fun was over and the crossness was about to begin.

Chapter Six

While Cally was making tea, Megan searched the bathroom for nail varnish remover. She couldn't find any, so she tried scrubbing the stain on her skirt with the nail brush and soap. But that didn't do any good. In fact the skirt looked even messier now because the soap had made the material go all stiff.

I'm sure it'll be OK if I dry it with Mum's hairdryer, thought Megan, going into her mum's room.

She plugged in the hairdryer and turned it right up, so the air that came out of it was very hot and strong, then she pointed it at the damp patch on her skirt.

The hairdryer was so noisy that Megan didn't notice her mum coming into the room, until she heard a cross voice behind her.

"Megan! What *are* you doing?"

Megan jumped. "Nothing."

"Of course you're doing something. What's this on your skirt? Turn the hairdryer off!"

Megan did as she was told. Her mum's voice sounded even crosser in the quiet room. "How did that nail varnish get there?"

"Lily spilt it." The moment Megan had spoken she wished she hadn't.

Her mum's lips were pursed. "I see.

And would this be the same Lily who Cally tells me you rolled down the hill with?"

Megan nodded. So her mum had seen the grass stains. "It wasn't Lily's fault. It was *my* idea, you see."

"What? To roll down the hill or to paint your nails?"

"Both."

"Hm." Megan's mum was still looking cross. "And did Lily choose the top that Cally's just shown me?"

Megan was about to say yes, when she realised that her mum was trying to catch her out, so she shook her head.

"Are you sure? Because Cally said she thought you would have been perfectly happy with a nice flowery top if Lily hadn't said she preferred the other one."

Megan's mum was looking right into

Megan's eyes. It was impossible to tell a lie. But if she told the truth it would make Lily seem like a naughty girl when she wasn't one at all.

"Lily said she liked it better than the other one. But that's not why I bought it."

"Well, it seems to me that something always goes wrong when Lily's around. I couldn't believe it when I saw those terrible green stains on your brand new T-shirt. And now you've got nail varnish all over your school clothes. I'll never get those marks off, you know." Megan bit her lip and wondered what to say, but her mum carried on. "I *had* been thinking of inviting Lily for tea this week, but I've changed my mind now."

Megan was suddenly desperate for Lily to come to tea. Then her mum would see what a nice girl she was.

"Oh pleeeeease, Mum! Pleeeeease can she come? I promise we'll be as good as the goodest girls in the world."

"If she *does* come, this will be your last chance to prove you can behave when you're together."

"We'll be better than angels!" said Megan, jumping up and tugging on her mum's hand. "So pleeeeease, can she come tomorrow?"

"I'll have to see what Cally says."

At that moment Cally called up the stairs that she was just going.

"Mum says is it OK for Lily to come to tea tomorrow?" asked Megan, before her mum could change her mind.

"OK by me. I'll give Jules a ring and sort it out if you want."

Megan closed her eyes tight, screwed up her face and held her breath, waiting to see what her mum would say.

"I'll leave it with you then, Cally."

"Yesss!" said Megan, opening her eyes and punching the air. "Thanks, Mum!"

Chapter Seven

"This is the kitchen," said Megan, standing in the middle of the room and twirling round.

"Calm down, you're getting overexcited," said Cally.

Megan was too happy, that Lily had come for tea, to calm down. "I'll show you all the rooms, shall I?"

Lily nodded happily and followed Megan out of the kitchen and into the living room.

When Megan had shown Lily all the rooms downstairs she showed her upstairs, finishing with her own bedroom.

"I like your bed!" said Lily. "It's miles bigger than mine."

"It's good for singing and dancing on," said Megan, handing Lily a plastic microphone. "I'll show you. You can have the proper microphone and I'll have a hairbrush."

"I'm not very good at singing or dancing," said Lily.

"Me neither," said Megan, putting a CD on. "It doesn't matter. It's just good fun wobbling around."

Megan got up on to the bed. Suddenly she found she was thinking about Georgie.

"I've got a sort of friend called Georgie," she told Lily. "Only I haven't seen her for ages because she goes to another school. I once saw her dancing on a stage though, like this."

The loud music began and Megan started bending her knees and punching her arms into the air.

"You *do* look funny," giggled Lily.

"I know. I can't dance for toffee!" said Megan. "But it's good fun, isn't it?" She sang some made-up words loudly, holding the hairbrush like a microphone, while Lily giggled even more. "Come on, Lily. *You* have a go."

Lily was too shy to sing but she bounced about and punched her arms in the air. Megan absolutely loved dancing with Lily. They were having such a good time they only just heard Cally call up the stairs, "I hope you two are behaving yourselves."

Megan turned the music down and

went to her door. "We're dancing. It's good fun!" she said.

"All right," said Cally. "I'll call you when tea's ready."

When Megan went back into her room the most wicked idea came into her head.

"Come with me!" she said, grabbing Lily's hand and tiptoeing out on to the landing. "Only don't let Cally hear us or she'll stop the fun."

"Is this your mum and dad's room?" asked Lily, in scarcely more than a whisper, as they crept inside the room and shut the door.

"Yes, and this is where Mum keeps her really posh party dresses."

Lily's eyes widened. Megan thought this was even better than showing Lily the house. She opened the door

of the biggest wardrobe.

"Oh wow!" breathed Lily, when she saw the beautiful dresses hanging up.

Megan reached up and slid a dark green dress off its hanger. "Here, you have this one." Lily gasped. Megan beamed. "And I'll have this red one."

"We're not going to put them on, are we?" asked Lily, in a breathy whisper.

Megan nodded, her eyes dancing.

“Are we allowed?” Lily squeaked.

Megan didn’t answer. She was too busy stroking the top of the red dress. “It’s velvet! Feel! And look! Yours has got all those sparkly sequins!”

“I know!” said Lily, in an even higher squeak. Her eyes were still enormous. “And what about these sticky-out petticoats! Your mum must look like a queen when she dresses up in these!”

Megan didn’t reply. She was too busy

changing into the red dress.

"Are you sure it's all right?" asked Lily. "What if Cally comes up?"

"She'll be ages making tea, and she'll probably give Beth hers at the same time." Megan turned round. "Can you do my zip up?"

Lily couldn't help giggling. "It's miles too big for you!"

Megan walked round the room pretending to be a model. She held the skirt high to stop it trailing on the floor. "Try yours on, Lily. Come on!"

Lily's was even longer than Megan's, but so beautiful. "I feel like a fairy princess!" she said.

"Stand on the bed!" said Megan, clambering up clumsily. "Let's pretend we're on the balcony at the grandest palace in the world, and we're waving to all the people. I'm called Princess Savanna. What's your name?"

Lily struggled to get up on the bed. She kept on putting her knee on the material and getting stuck. "Princess Anastasia," she said. Then she giggled as she collapsed in the middle of the bed.

That made Megan lose her balance and fall on top of Lily.

"Get off!" laughed Lily. "You're squashing me!"

But Megan had such a big fit of the giggles that she couldn't move. "You're getting my dress all crushed!" spluttered Lily. Suddenly, there was a ripping noise. And that was when the door opened.

Both girls froze. Megan gasped and Lily hid her face.

In the doorway stood Megan's mum. "What *do* you think you're doing?" she said in a low angry voice.

Megan couldn't speak. She was too shocked. If only she could wake up and find it was all a bad dream.

Lily wasn't hiding her face any more but she looked terrified.

"I'm going to ask Cally to take Lily straight home," said Megan's mum, her voice still shaking with anger. "There's *always* trouble when you two get together – so from now on, you're not to see each other again."

The next few days were the most miserable of Megan's life. She tried to explain to her mum that it wasn't Lily's idea to try on the dresses. "And it was *my* foot that tore the green dress, not Lily's. Honestly!"

But her mum just got angry again.

"Who were you with when you got grass stains all over your clothes? Lily! Who were you with when you nearly ruined my best dresses? Lily. Who spilled nail varnish on your school skirt? Lily! And don't think I didn't notice those tattoos! I suppose that was Lily's idea too?"

"Yes, but—"

"But nothing!"

By the weekend, Megan missed Lily like mad. She didn't dare mention her name, though, in case her mum turned angry again. The worst thing of all was that Megan's tattoo had completely faded away. It felt as though Lily had faded out of her life.

On Saturday afternoon Megan went to the park with Mum, Dad and Beth.

"Swing me again!" said Beth, holding hands with her mum and dad.

"Not another one!" said her dad.

"Last one!" said her mum.

"Wheeeee!" shouted Beth, as her parents swung her up in the air.

"Look!" said Megan. "There's a puppet show over there!"

"Puppets, Bethy!" said her mum. "Let's go and see."

"Puppets!" repeated Beth at the top of her voice, tugging on her mum's hand.

Then Megan spotted something even more interesting. "Wow! Jugglers!" she said. "Can I go and watch them?"

"Hello, you lot," said a voice behind them. "Long time no see!"

Megan glanced round. It was one of her mum and dad's friends. They all started chatting.

"Mum, can I watch the jugglers?" Megan asked again. "They're only just there."

"Yes, but come back here in a minute."

So Megan rushed off to the small crowd of people watching them. She stared wide-eyed as the jugglers threw *five* clubs to each other, keeping them all in the air at the same time. Then one of the men took his shoe off, without dropping any clubs, and the next minute they were throwing the shoe backwards and forwards as well. It was so cool. The audience laughed and clapped like mad.

Megan wanted her mum and dad to see how good the juggling was. She looked over to the puppet theatre. There was no sign of her mum or Beth. But her dad was there. Only something was the matter. He looked really worried.

Megan ran over to him, her heart beating fast.

"Beth's disappeared," said her dad, in a shaky voice.

Megan gasped.

★★★

Chapter Nine

"Stay right here!" said Megan's dad, pointing to all the children watching the puppet show. "I'm going to help Mum look. If you spot Beth, hang on to her and don't move."

Megan felt sick. She looked at all the little children near her. None of them was Beth. Then she looked around as far as she could see. There were so many people everywhere – but no Beth.

A couple of minutes later her mum

appeared, frantic with worry.

"Do you want me to help search, Mum?"

"No. You stay put. I don't want to lose you as well."

Megan watched her mum running off in the direction of the little train.

It wasn't till she was out of earshot that Megan thought of something. Of course! The ducks! That was where Beth would be.

Behind Megan, Punch and Judy argued with each other in loud squeaky voices, while the audience laughed and called things out. But Megan just stared around. A terrible thought had come into her head. What if Beth walked too near to the edge of the duck pond?

Her heart was hurting, it was beating so hard. She wanted to run to the duck

pond as fast as she could to make sure Beth was safe. But her mum had told her to stay put. If she came back and found Megan missing too, she'd be even more worried.

Megan bit her lip as lots of thoughts went whizzing through her head. If she *did* manage to find Beth, her mum would be too happy to be cross, wouldn't she? But what if Beth *wasn't* at the duck pond? What if Beth was trying to find her way back to the puppets, and when she got there, she couldn't see Megan because Megan had gone?

No, Megan had better do as she was told and stay put. She shivered as her eyes darted all over the place. Her mum and dad had been gone for ages. If only one of them would come back so she could tell them where to look.

Inside Megan's head flashed a terrible picture of Beth walking too near to the edge of the duck pond and falling in.

If Mum or Dad doesn't come back in one minute, I'm going to go and look, thought Megan, shutting her eyes tight for a moment to make the time go faster.

When she opened them, like magic, her mum and dad were rushing back towards her.

"Have you seen her?" called her mum, all white-faced.

"No," said Megan. "But I bet she's by the duck pond. She loves the ducks."

"Let's go," said her dad, grabbing Megan's hand and breaking into a run.

Then all three of them stopped in their tracks and just stared. Coming towards them, wearing a huge smile, was Beth. She was holding someone's hand.

"Lily!" said Megan's mum in a low, angry voice. "I might have known." Megan felt as though she was frozen to the spot. Then her mum rushed forwards and scooped up Beth, cuddling her close.

"See'd ducks!" said Beth, trying to wriggle out of the tight hug.

Lily's eyes were as round as ever in her pale face. "I saw Beth by the duck pond," she said softly. "She seemed to be all on her own and I was worried about her. I told her to come and help me find her mummy."

There was a silence, then Megan's dad spoke.

"Well done, Lily. You did exactly the right thing."

Megan didn't feel quite so much like a statue after her dad had spoken. She looked at her mum. She was still cuddling

Beth, but her eyes had changed. They weren't cross any more. In fact she was looking at Lily in a very different way. Only Lily didn't see because she was staring at the ground.

"I'd better go back to Jules now," she said, turning to go.

Megan noticed Jules hurrying towards them. Any minute now Lily would be gone again.

"Lily," said Megan's mum in a gentle voice, "I happen to know there's a café in town where they sell lovely creamy éclairs. Why don't you ask Jules if you can both come and have tea with us?"

Megan couldn't believe what she was hearing. A little bubble of happiness was floating about inside her.

Lily turned and looked straight at Megan's mum. Her eyes were puzzled.

"I want to thank you for bringing Beth back, Lily," said Megan's mum. "I'm so pleased Megan's got a friend like you."

Lily went pink. And just then a familiar voice called out from over near the jugglers. "Jules! I've been looking for you everywhere!" It was Cally.

Megan's mum smiled and beckoned her over. "We're just off to the café for chocolate éclairs. Come and join us!" Then she put one arm round Lily and the other round Megan.

Cally stopped in her tracks and stared.

"You'd better hurry," called Megan's mum. Her voice dropped to a whisper so only Megan and Lily could hear. "After all, we want to leave enough time to go to the shops afterwards, don't we? You two need a new tattoo each. Let's hope they've still got some of those knots."

That was when Lily's face stopped looking puzzled and broke into one of her great big beams. And suddenly Megan had the strangest feeling. A back to front feeling. A feeling that the crossness was over – and the fun was about to begin!

Look out for...

Lily wants to help her new friend – but can she come up with the perfect plan?

Make Friends With

1	Chloe ★ Jessica	1 84121 734 4	£3.99 ☐
2	Georgie ★ Megan	1 84121 784 0	£3.99 ☐
3	Lily ★ Izzie	1 84121 786 7	£3.99 ☐
4	Claire ★ Lauren	1 84121 790 5	£3.99 ☐
5	Yasmin ★ Lucy	1 84121 792 1	£3.99 ☐
6	Rachel ★ Zoe	1 84121 794 8	£3.99 ☐
7	Jade ★ Amy	1 84121 796 4	£3.99 ☐
8	Hannah ★ Poppy	1 84121 798 0	£3.99 ☐

Make Friends With books are available from all good bookshops,
or can be ordered direct from the publisher:
Orchard Books, PO BOX 29, Douglas IM99 1BQ
Credit card orders please telephone 01624 836000
or fax 01624 837033
or e-mail: bookshop@enterprise.net for details.

To order please quote title, author and ISBN
and your full name and address.
Cheques and postal orders should be made payable to
'Bookpost plc.'
Postage and packing is FREE within the UK
(overseas customers should add £1.00 per book).

Prices and availability are subject to change.

Coming up next in...

Make Friends With Megan

Megan can't keep out of trouble – is it because of her new best friend?